Spooky Friends

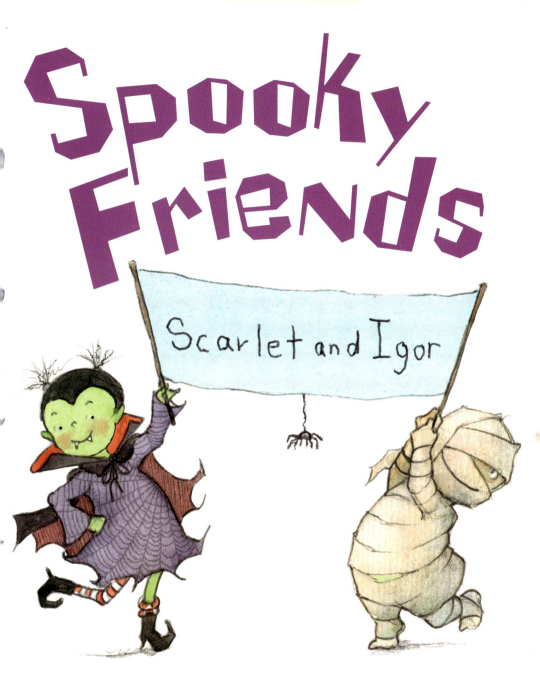

Scarlet and Igor

by JANE FEDER

illustrated by JULIE DOWNING

SCHOLASTIC PRESS / NEW YORK

For Neal who inspired it, Julie who brought it to life,

and Dianne who made it happen — J.F.

To Jane, Dianne, and Marijka with thanks — J.D.

Text copyright © 2013 by Jane Feder • Illustrations copyright © 2013 by Julie Downing

Library of Congress Cataloging-in-Publication Data
Feder, Jane. Spooky friends / by Jane Feder ; illustrated by Julie Downing.
— 1st ed. p. cm. — (Spooky friends)
Summary: Scarlet the vampire and Igor the mummy are best friends, even though they can never agree on anything. But when they cooperate, wonderful things begin to happen.

ISBN 978-0-545-47815-1 (hardcover : alk. paper) — ISBN 978-0-545-47816-8 (pbk. : alk. paper) 1. Vampires—Juvenile fiction. 2. Mummies—Juvenile fiction. 3. Best friends—Juvenile fiction. 4. Friendship—Juvenile fiction. [1. Vampires—Fiction. 2. Mummies—Fiction. 3. Best friends—Fiction. 4. Friendship—Fiction.] I. Downing, Julie, ill. II. Title. PZ7.F2997Spo 2013[E]—dc23 2012014786

10 9 8 7 6 5 4 3 2 1   13 14 15 16 17
Printed in China   38
First edition, August 2013

The display type was set in Brickhouse. The text was set in Adobe Garamond Pro Regular. The art was created with ballpoint pen, watercolor, and digital artwork. Book design by Marijka Kostiw

Table of Contents

Scarlet and Igor

Scarlet and Igor were very good friends.

The trouble was, they could never agree on anything.

If Scarlet said, "Up!"

Igor said, "Down!"

When Igor made a short snowman,

Scarlet made hers tall.

If Igor wanted to read,

Scarlet wanted to sing.

If Scarlet wanted to nap,

Igor wanted to dance.

When Igor made a tall tower,

Scarlet made it short.

Igor got mad at Scarlet.

So he played all by himself.

And Scarlet got mad at Igor,

so she played all by herself.

After a while, Scarlet got lonely.

"Igor," she yelled, "I'm hungry!
Let's have gooseberry-jelly sandwiches."

"I'm hungry, too!" Igor yelled back.

"Let's have chestnut-butter sandwiches."

13

"Gooseberry-jelly sandwiches!"
yelled Scarlet.

"Chestnut butter!" yelled Igor.

"Gooseberry jelly!"

"Chestnut butter!"

"Gooseberry jelly!"

"Chestnut butter!"

15

"I know!" they said together.

"Let's have gooseberry-jelly-*AND*-chestnut-butter sandwiches. Yum!"

"Igor," said Scarlet, "I think we are very good friends."

"I think we are, too," said Igor.

And on that they could agree.

Scarlet and Igor Pick a Name

One night, Scarlet and Igor could not find Cat.

"We must look in the cellar," said Igor.

"We must look in the attic," said Scarlet.

They looked and looked and looked.

Then they heard Cat call, *"Meow!"*

20

"Scarlet," said Igor, "Cat had a kitten."

"Goody!" said Scarlet. "Let's pick a name."

Scarlet and Igor thought. . . .

"I know," said Igor. "Kitten's name
should be Echo."

"Oh, no!" said Scarlet. "It should be
Trinket."

"No, no!" said Igor. "Let's call it Fang."

"Ember," said Scarlet.

"Bax!" said Igor.

"Jinx!" said Scarlet.

"Spooky!" yelled Igor.

"Velvet!" yelled Scarlet.

"Look, Scarlet," said Igor.

"Cat is bringing us Kitten!"

"And she's bringing another
kitten," said Scarlet.

"And another kitten," said Igor.

"And another kitten," said Scarlet and
Igor together.

"And another kitten and another kitten

and another kitten and another kitten."

Igor and Scarlet watched the new little kittens—Echo, Trinket, Fang, Ember, Bax, Jinx, Spooky, and Velvet.

"Scarlet," said Igor, "we are very good at picking names."

"Yes, we are," agreed Scarlet.

"Meow!" said Cat.

Which meant she thought so, too.

Scarlet and Igor Make Pictures

"Let's draw," said Scarlet.

"No!" said Igor. "Let's paint."

"Draw!"

"Paint!"

"Draw!"

"Paint!"

So Igor took the paints
and Scarlet took the crayons.

"Look, Igor," said Scarlet.
"I am drawing a perfect square."

"So what?" said Igor. "I am painting a pointy triangle."

"Big deal," said Scarlet. "I drew a circle!"

"Who cares?" said Igor. "I painted a star!"

"BORING!" said Scarlet.

"I drew a tree with branches!"

"Look, Igor," said Scarlet.

"We made a house."

"A house with a tree," said Igor.

"No, look," said Scarlet.
"A house with a tree
and a moon."

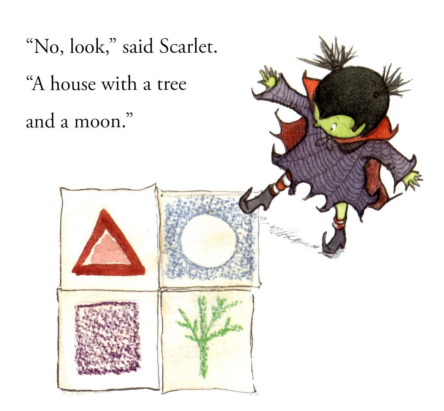

"A house with a tree and a moon
and a star," said Igor.

"Scarlet," said Igor. "There is a big empty place."

"Yes, there is," said Scarlet.

Scarlet and Igor looked at the empty place.

Then they looked at each other.

And together they made a picture of . . .

Scarlet and Igor!